J.D. Runkle

The Mathematical Monthly

May, 1859

SALZWASSER
VERLAG

J.D. Runkle

The Mathematical Monthly

May, 1859

Reprint of the original, first published in 1859.

1st Edition 2023 | ISBN: 978-3-37513-820-2

Verlag (Publisher): Salzwasser Verlag GmbH, Zeilweg 44, 60439 Frankfurt, Deutschland
Vertretungsberechtigt (Authorized to represent): E. Roepke, Zeilweg 44, 60439 Frankfurt, Deutschland
Druck (Print): Books on Demand GmbH, In de Tarpen 42, 22848 Norderstedt, Deutschland

Price Twenty-Five Cents.

Vol. I.   No. VIII.

THE

MATHEMATICAL MONTHLY.

MAY, 1859.

EDITED BY

J. D. RUNKLE, A.M., A.A.S.

CAMBRIDGE:

PUBLISHED BY JOHN BARTLETT.

LONDON:

TRÜBNER AND CO.

1859.

CONTENTS.

MAY, 1859.

TERMS.

A single Copy,	$3.00 per annum.
Two Copies to one Address,	5.00 "
Five Copies " "	11.00 "
Ten Copies " "	20.00 "

Payable invariably in advance.

JOHN BARTLETT. *Publisher*.

CAMBRIDGEPORT:

W. F. Brown, Book and Job Printer, 421 Main Street.

PRESS OF H. O. HOUGHTON & CO.

THE

MATHEMATICAL MONTHLY.

Vol. I... M A Y, 1859.... No. VIII.

PRIZE PROBLEMS FOR STUDENTS.

I.

IF x be the distance of the eye from the centre of a sphere, of which the radius is r, prove that the visible part of its surface is to the invisible as $x - r : x + r$.

II.

Transpose the series

$$1 + 8 + 19 + 34 + 53 + 76 + \&c.,$$

so as to find the sum of n terms by means of the usual formula for summing the squares of the natural numbers.

III.

If a, b, c are the sides of a spherical triangle, and A, B, C the opposite angles, prove that

$$\sin b \sin c + \cos b \cos c \cos A = \sin B \sin C - \cos B \cos C \cos a.$$

IV.

If, on the sides of a given plane triangle, equilateral triangles be constructed, prove that the triangle formed by joining the centres of these equilateral triangles will also be equilateral; also prove that the straight lines joining the vertices of the equilateral triangles and the opposite angles of the given triangle are equal, and all intersect in the same point.

V.

If an angle (A), and the sum of the squares of the sides of a plane triangle, be given ($= 8\,a^2$), prove that the curve which continually bisects the side opposite to A is an ellipse, and determine the numerical values of its principal diameters when $A = 60°$, and $a = 10$.

The solution of these problems must be received by the first of July, 1859.

REPORT OF THE JUDGES UPON THE SOLUTIONS OF THE PRIZE PROBLEMS IN No. IV., Vol. I.

THE first Prize is awarded to WILLIAM E. MERRILL, Cadet, First Class United States Military Academy, West Point, N. Y.

The second Prize is awarded to W. F. OSBORNE, Sophomore Class, Wesleyan University, Middletown, Ct.

PRIZE SOLUTION OF PROBLEM I.

"If the triangle DEF be inscribed in the triangle ABC, the circumferences of the circles circumscribed about the three triangles AEF, BFD, CDE, will pass through the same point."

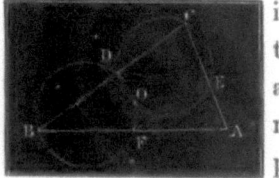

Let the circles described about the triangles BFD and DCE intersect at the point O. Connect O with the vertices D, E, F of the inscribed triangle. Since the angle FOD is the supplement of B, and the angle EOD is the supplement of C, ∴ the angle $FOE = B + C$. Adding A to both sides, we have $FOE + A = B + C + A = 180°$. ∴ O is on the circumference of the circle circumscribing the triangle AEF. This solution is by W. F. OSBORNE.

PRIZE SOLUTION OF PROBLEM II.

" Given the base of a spherical triangle, and the ratio of the tangents of the angles at the base ; to find the locus of the vertex." — Communicated by GEORGE EAST-WOOD, Esq.

Let ABC be the triangle. Refer the vertex C to the base by the perpendicular CD. Denote the base by a, and AD by x; DB will be denoted by $a-x$. From the triangles ADC and CDB, Napier's Circular Parts give

$$\sin x = \tan CD \cot A, \quad \sin (a-x) = \tan CD \cot B.$$

$$\therefore \frac{\sin (a-x)}{\sin x} = \frac{\tan CD \cot B}{\tan CD \cot A} = \frac{\tan A}{\tan B} = m = \text{given ratio.}$$

$$\therefore \quad m \sin x = \sin (a-x)$$

$$= \sin a \cos x - \cos a \sin x,$$

$$\therefore \sin x (m + \cos a) = \sin a \cos x,$$

$$\therefore \sin^2 x (m + \cos a)^2 = \sin^2 a \cos^2 x = \sin^2 a (1 - \sin^2 x),$$

$$\therefore \sin^2 x (m^2 + 2m \cos a + 1) = \sin^2 a,$$

$$\therefore \qquad \sin x = \frac{\pm \sin a}{\sqrt{(m^2 + 2m \cos a + 1)}} = \text{a constant.}$$

Hence AD is constant for all positions of the vertex C, and the required locus is therefore a great circle perpendicular to the base. If $m = 1$, $x = \frac{1}{2}a$; that is, the base is bisected by the locus. This solution is by WILLIAM E. MERRILL.

PRIZE SOLUTION OF PROBLEM III.

" If in any triangle a line be drawn from the vertex of either angle to the oppo-site side, bisecting the angle, prove that the product of this line and the secant of half the bisected angle equals a harmonic mean between the two sides containing the bisected angle." — Communicated by Prof. J. M. VANVLECK.)

Let the angle ABC, which is bisected by BD, equal 2θ. Then the area of the triangle $ABD = \frac{1}{2}AB \times BD \sin \theta$; the area of $CBD = \frac{1}{2}BC \times BD \sin \theta$; the area of $ABC = \frac{1}{2}AB \times BC \sin 2\theta$.

$$\therefore \frac{1}{2}BC \times BD \sin \theta + \frac{1}{2}AB \times BD \sin \theta = \frac{1}{2}AB \times BC \sin 2\theta,$$

$$\therefore (BC + AB)\, BD \sin \theta = AB \times BC \sin 2\theta$$
$$= 2\, AB \times BC \sin \theta \cos \theta,$$
$$\therefore \qquad BD \sec \theta = \frac{2\, AB \times BC}{AB + BC}.$$

This solution is by ASHER B. EVANS. The problem was solved in the same manner by W. L. OSBORNE.

PRIZE SOLUTION OF PROBLEM IV.

"If A, B, C, and D be any four points in the same plane, so situated that four circles, ABC, ABD, ACD, and BCD, can be drawn through them three and three, prove that the circumferences of any two of these circles will intersect at the same angle as the circumferences of the remaining two." — Communicated by Prof. H. A. NEWTON.

Let A, B, C, D be the four points, joined by straight lines, two

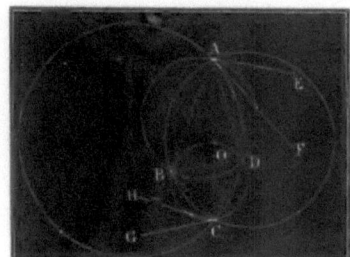

and two. Since each of these lines is a common chord to two of the circles, and since the angle formed by a tangent and a chord is equal to the inscribed angle measured by the same arc, we have $ABD = DAE$ and $ACD = DAF$. $\therefore ABD - ACD = DAE - DAF = FAE =$ the angle made by two of the circumferences.

Again, $BDC = BCG$, and $BAC = BCH$.

$\therefore BDC - BAC = BCG - BCH = HCG$.

But $AOD = BAC + ABD = ACD + BDC$.

$\therefore ABD - ACD = BDC - BAC = FAE = HCG$.

In precisely the same way the proposition may be proved for any other circumferences two and two.

It is evident that either point, as D, may fall within the triangle formed by joining the other three points; but it will not be difficult to modify the figure, and prove the proposition for this case. This solution is by W. F. Osborne.

Prize Solution of Problem V.

"A paraboloid of given dimensions but unknown specific gravity is immersed in common water, until its summit coincides with the surface of the fluid. The pressure from above being removed, the body ascends by the force of the water until its base coincides with the fluid's surface, and then descends, and so on. Find from this circumstance the specific gravity of the body." — Communicated by George East-wood, Esq.

Let BAC represent a vertical section of the paraboloid through its axis AD. Let $AN=x$, $EN=y$, $AD = a$, $BD=b$. Then from a property of the parabola $b^2 : y^2 :: a : x$. Whence $y^2 = \frac{b^2 x}{a}$. Let ENF represent the surface of the water at any instant. Then the amount of water displaced equals the solidity of the frustrum

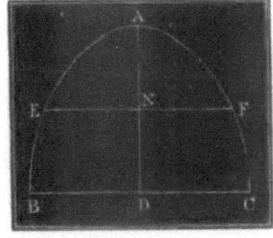

$$EBCF = ABC - AEF = \tfrac{1}{2}\pi b^2 a - \tfrac{1}{2}\pi y^2 x = \frac{\pi b^2}{2a}(a^2 - x^2).$$

Let $g =$ the specific gravity of the paraboloid, then its weight, water being the standard unit, $= \frac{\pi}{2} b^2 a g$. Then

$$\frac{\pi b^2}{2a}(a^2 - x^2) - \frac{\pi}{2} b^2 a g = \frac{\pi b^2}{2a}(a^2 - x^2 - a^2 g) = F = \text{the force tending}$$

to elevate the paraboloid at any instant. If the summit A was at the surface of the water when the ascent commenced, the space $s = AN = x$. Let $v =$ the velocity due to the space s; then, since the accelerating force is variable, we have $F ds = m v dv$; m denoting the mass of the paraboloid.

Substituting for F and s their values as found above, we have

$$\frac{\pi b^2}{2a}(a^2 - x^2 - a^2 g)\,dx = m v dv.$$

Integrating $\quad \dfrac{\pi b^2}{2a}(a^2 - a^2 g)\,x - \dfrac{\pi b^2}{2a}\cdot\dfrac{x^3}{3} = \tfrac{1}{2} m v^2.$

As $v = 0$ when $x = a$, we have

$$\frac{\pi b^3}{2a}(a^2 - a^2 g) a - \frac{\pi b^2}{2a} \cdot \frac{a^3}{3} = 0.$$

Whence, from this equation, $g = \frac{2}{3}$ of the specific gravity of water. This solution is by ASHER B. EVANS.

JOSEPH WINLOCK.
CHAUNCEY WRIGHT.
TRUMAN HENRY SAFFORD.

THE CONIC SECTION COMPASSES.

By JOSEPH P. FRIZELL, Lowell, Mass.

THE frequency with which the ellipse, parabola, and hyperbola occur in architecture and mechanics, the extensive applications of which they are capable in the solution and illustration of algebraical and geometrical questions, and their many interesting properties, which can be fully appreciated only when they are correctly drawn, render an instrument which describes them with readiness and precision, a valuable addition to our present stock of mathematical apparatus.

The instrument represented in the accompanying drawing is designed to effect this object, which it does by virtue of the well-known property which gives to these curves the name of conic sections. I shall first describe the instrument, and, next, indicate the theoretical considerations on which its operation depends. M is a heavy rectangular block of metal with two beveled edges, the weight of which serves to keep the instrument in its position. At right angles to the plane of its base is fixed the vertical pillar S, which is graduated to inches and twentieths upon its face fg. Upon this pillar slides vertically the disc F, capable of being fixed at any height, by means of a clamp screw, the nonius or index whereby it is thus adjusted coinciding, in vertical height, with the point c. On the face of the disc, next the pillar, is graduated an arc of ninety degrees, the centre of which is at c, and its zero in a horizontal line passing through c. Upon the front face of this disc

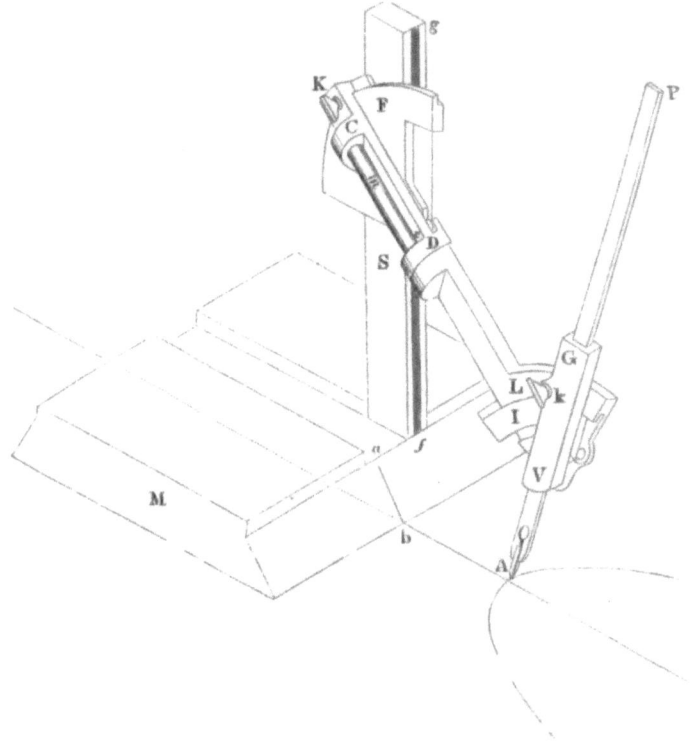

Fig. 1.

is fixed the guide CD, which radiates about the centre c, and is adjustable upon the disc at any angle of the quadrant, by means of an index, vernier, and clamp screw at R. Two lugs, formed upon this guide at C and D, embrace the axis or journal, m, which revolves in the lugs, and is capable of no other motion. This axis is extended beyond the guide CD; and upon its extension is formed another small disc, L. To this disc is jointed another guide, GV, radiating about the point V, which is in a straight line passing through c and the index at K. The guide GV may be adjusted, at any angle, to the axis KV by a clamp screw k and a limb I fitting into a corresponding groove in the disc L; the united length of the limb and groove being, if necessary, available, thereby allowing of any inclination GVK from near zero to ninety degrees. A perfectly straight rod or ruler, AP, carrying a pencil at its extremity A, is fitted to slide accurately, but with as little resistance as possible, through the guide GV; its central line passing through the point V. It must be observed, that by the point V is meant the point where the short axis, around which GV radiates, is intersected by the axis of the cylindrical journal m produced; and that by the point c is meant the point where the axis around which CD radiates is intersected by the axis of m. On each edge of the block M is marked a line coinciding with a vertical plane passing through the points V and c; b being vertically under c.

Suppose, now, the instrument to be standing upon a table or drawing board, the point A of the pencil touching the surface of the paper. If the journal m be made to revolve, carrying around the rod PA, this latter will generate the two nappes of a cone having its vertex at V. If, during such revolution, the rod PA be slipped through the guide so as to keep the point of the pencil in contact with the paper, it will describe a conic section determined in species, magnitude, and position, by (1) the angle at which the index K is placed upon the disc F; (2) the angle made by the generatrix PA with the axis; (3) the position of the point V.

I proceed to the theoretical considerations which indicate the method of adjusting the instrument so as to draw any given curve.

Two questions present themselves in this connection: namely, (1) What conditions must a plane satisfy, in order that its intersection with a given cone may be a given curve? (2) What conditions must a cone satisfy, in order that its intersection with a fixed plane may be a given curve? To solve the first: Suppose a cone, in which v represents the angle at the base, to be intersected at a distance a from the vertex (measured on the slant side) by a plane, making an angle u with the base. The general equation of the curve of intersection will be

$$(1) \qquad y^2 = 2\,a\,x \cot v \sin(v+u) - x^2 \left(1 - \frac{\sin^2 u}{\sin^2 v}\right)$$

in which the curve is referred to its vertex and transverse axis.

The general equation of a conic section, referred to its vertex and transverse axis, is

$$(2) \qquad y^2 = 2\,m\,x\,(1+e) - x^2\,(1-e^2)$$

where m is the distance from the focus to the vertex, and e is the eccentricity. Therefore, by the principle of indeterminate coefficients $1 - \frac{\sin^2 u}{\sin^2 v} = 1 - e^2$, and $2\,a \cot v \sin(v+u) = 2\,m\,(1+e)$. Therefore, $\sin u = e \sin v$ (3), and $a = \frac{m\,(1+e)}{\cot v \sin(v+u)}$ (4), which are the required conditions.

The solution of the second question is contained in the two following propositions.

(1) If a sphere be enveloped by a cone whose surface is intersected by a plane tangent to the sphere, the point of tangency is a focus of the section.

(2) The locus of the vertices of all the right cones whose intersection with a given plane is a given curve, is a conic section, having its vertices at the foci, and its foci at the vertices of the given curve; its plane being perpendicular to the given plane, and intersecting it in the transverse axis. If the given curve be an ellipse, the locus is an hyperbola; if an hyperbola, the locus is an ellipse;

if a parabola, the locus is also a parabola. Both these properties are readily deduced from Equation (3); and, when I began to write this article, I was not aware that the second proposition had ever been stated before. I have since found them both in the *Cambridge Philosophical Transactions*, Vol. III., Part 1, Memoir 8, where they seem to be claimed as original discoveries by PIERCE MORTON. A reference to this authority renders a demonstration unnecessary.

These properties will be more readily understood from an ex-

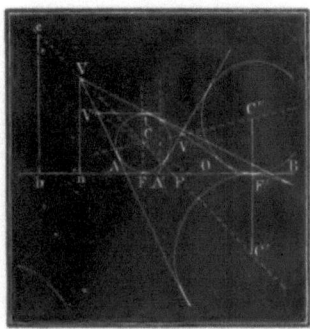

Fig. 2.

amination of Fig. 2, which is supposed to be an axial section of a cone or system of cones; *A B* being the projection of a cutting plane, and the circles tangent at *F, F'*, sections of the inscribed spheres.

The curve of intersection may be regarded as an ellipse whose vertices are *A, B*, and foci *F, F'*; an hyperbola whose vertices are *A', B'*, and foci *F, F'*; or a parabola whose vertex is *A* and focus *F*. In the first case, the vertex of the cone is at *V*; in the second at *V'*; in the third at *V''*. By supposing the circle tangent at *F* to vary in magnitude, it is shown, in the first case, that the locus of *V* is an hyperbola having its foci at *A, B*, and its vertices at *F, F'*; in the second case, that the locus of *V'* is an ellipse having its vertices at *F, F'* and its foci at *A', B'*; in the third case, that the locus of *V''* is a parabola, having its vertex at *F* and focus at *A*. It is obvious that the axis of the cone is tangent to the locus at *V V' V''*, since, in the case of the ellipse and hyperbola, it makes equal angles with lines drawn from *V, V'* to the foci, and in the case of the parabola it bisects the angle formed by a line to the focus, and a perpendicular upon the directrix.

These properties indicate the method of adjusting the instrument so as to draw any given conic section. From the equation of the given curve, or from the data by which it is given, the equation of the corresponding locus must be found. Any convenient point in this locus being chosen by assuming one of its coördinates, and finding the other from its equation, the angle which a tangent to the locus at that point makes with the transverse axis must be found. This angle must be laid off on the disc F. The point V in the instrument must be placed at the point chosen in the locus. The inclination $G\,V\,K$ must then be made such that the point A of the pencil shall touch the vertex of the given curve. The instrument is then ready to draw the curve.

As an example of this operation, let it be required to draw an ellipse whose semi-transverse axis is $A\,O$, and whose semi-focal distance is $F\,O$. We are first to find the angle to be laid off on the disc F. This may be done in either of two ways. (1) Let the equation of the locus of V be formed, which will be $A^2 y^2 - B^2 x^2 = A^2 B^2$, in which $A^2 = A\,O^2, B^2 = A\,O^2 - F\,O^2$, and x, y are the general coördinates. In this locus choose any convenient point to be occupied by V (Fig. 1). Designate its coördinates by $x'y', y'$ being any assumed distance Vn, and $x' = \sqrt{A^2 + \frac{A^2}{B^2}y'^2}$. The equation of a tangent to the locus at V is $A^2 y y' - B^2 x x' = -A^2 B^2$, in which, if we make $y = 0$, we have $x = \frac{A^2}{x'}$. Make $O\,P = \frac{A^2}{x'}$, and through P draw VP. The angle $V\,P\,n$ is the angle required. (2) A very much simpler, though perhaps slightly less accurate, method of finding this angle, is by a geometrical construction indicated in the figure; thus, erect the perpendicular Ft, upon which with any convenient radius $C\,F$ draw a circle. From A and B draw tangents to this circle, and from V, their point of meeting, draw through C a line meeting, $A\,B$ in P. $V\,P\,n$ is the angle required, as before. The angle thus found must be laid off upon the disc F, and the axis clamped in that position by the thumbscrew K. Upon PV produced, take $Vc = VC$ (Fig. 1), and draw cb perpendicular to AB. Next, place the edge b of the instrument at b (Fig. 2), taking care to make the line ab, and its corresponding line on the opposite edge of the block M, coincide with the prolongation of the transverse axis. Elevate the disc F till its index is at a distance cb above the paper, in which position let it be clamped. Make the inclination of the generatrix to the axis such that A may touch the vertex of the curve, which can then be drawn.

If, from the great eccentricity of the ellipse, the pencil meets the paper near the opposite vertex, at too great an inclination to produce a definite line, one half the curve can be drawn, and then the instrument must be removed to a corresponding position on the opposite side of the centre to draw the other half.

In a manner entirely similar to that described for the ellipse, the instrument may be adjusted to draw either of the other conic sections.

ON CONTACT, CENTRES OF SIMILITUDE, AND RADICAL AXES.[*]

By MATTHEW COLLINS, B. A., Dublin, Ireland.

1. THE straight line joining the ends of any two parallel radii of two given circles passes through a fixed point in the line joining their centres; namely, the point where the distance of the centres is cut (externally or internally) in the ratio of the radii.

Let O and O' be the centres of two given circles, OC and $O'C'$ any pair of parallel radii, and P the point of intersection of CC'

---

[*] See Note at the end of this article.

and $O\,O'$; then as $O\,C$ is parallel to $O'\,C'$ ∴ the triangles $P\,O\,C$, $P\,O'\,C'$ are similar; therefore $P\,O:P\,O'=O\,C:O'\,C'$, and therefore constant; and as points O and O' are fixed, therefore P must be so too.

But if $O'\,C''$ be parallel and contrary to $O\,C$, then $O\,O'$ will obviously be cut internally by $C\,C''$ at P', in the ratio of the radii, so that

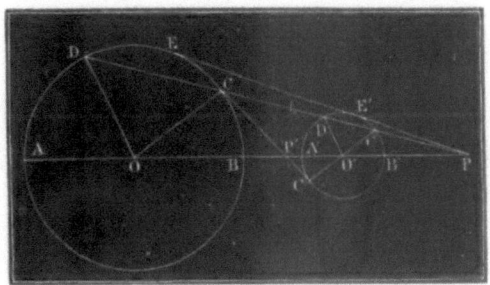

Fig. 1.

P' will be fixed as well as P, and $O\,O'$ will therefore be cut harmonically at P and P', which are called the external and internal centres of similitude of the two given circles.

CoROLLARY. Hence the point of contact of two circles is obviously their external or internal centre of similitude, according as the circles touch each other internally or externally; and a common tangent $E\,E'$ to two circles always passes through their centre of similitude, since the radii $O\,E$ and $O'\,E'$, passing through the points of contact E and E', are both perpendicular to the common tangent, and therefore parallel to each other.

2. If $O\,C$ be parallel to $O'\,C'$, then $O\,D$ must be parallel to $O'\,D'$, D and D' being the points where $C\,C'$ cuts the circles. Again, the angle $O\,D\,C=O\,C\,D=O'\,C'\,D'=O'\,D'\,C'$, and therefore $O\,D$ is parallel to $O'\,D'$; that is, D and D' will correspond if C and C' correspond.

3. Conversely, if from the centre of similitude P of two circles any line be drawn cutting them in C',D',C,D, so that C corresponds to C', then $P\,C\times P\,D'=P\,C'\times P\,D$ will be constant; and therefore $P\,B\times P\,A'=P\,A\times P\,B'=P\,E\times P\,E'$. For as C corresponds to C', $O\,C$ is parallel to $O'\,C'$, therefore $P\,C:P\,C'$ is con-

stant ($= O\,C : O'\,C'$), and as $P\,C' \times P\,D'$ is constant, therefore also $P\,C \times P\,D'$ is constant.

Obs. If the circles touch at B, A' will coincide with B, and the constant value of $P\,C \times P\,D'$ will then be $P\,B^2$.

4. By supposing one of the two given circles to become infinite, it follows that the centre of similitude of a straight line and circle is that point P on the circumference at the greatest (or least) distance from the given straight line and, moreover, that if through this point P any straight line be drawn cutting the given straight line and the circle in C and C', then $P\,C \times P\,C'$ will be constant, as is easily demonstrated otherwise, directly.

5. The radical axis of two circles is the locus of a point from which the tangents to the two given circles are equal to each other

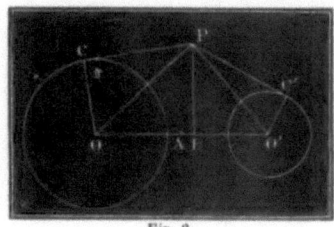

Fig. 2.

and is a straight line. For if the tangent $P\,C =$ the tangent $P\,C'$, O and O' being the centres, A the middle point of $O\,O'$, and $P\,B$ perpendicular to $O\,O'$, then $2\,O\,O' \times A\,B = P\,O^2 — P\,O'^2 \therefore = O\,C^2 — O'\,C'^2$; and as $O\,C$, $O'\,C'$, and $O\,O'$ are given, $\therefore AB$ is given, and therefore the point B is fixed, and so the locus of P is a straight line perpendicular to $O\,O'$ at B, when $O\,O'$ is divided, so that $O\,B^2 — O'\,B^2 = O\,C^2 — O'\,C'^2$.

Corollary. The radical axis of two circles that cut each other is their common chord, and the radical axis of two circles that touch each other is their common tangent at their point of contact, as is directly evident.

6. If a variable circle touch two fixed circles, the line joining the points of contact will pass through their centre of similitude, and the tangent from this centre to the variable circle will be constant.

Let the variable circle O'' touch the two fixed circles O and O'

at C and D', and let $C D'$
produced cut circle O'
and the line $O' O$ in C'
and P. Now $O O''$ and
$O' O''$ pass through C and
D', and angle $O' C' D' =$
angle $O' D' C'$ $\therefore$ = angle $O'' D' C$ $\therefore$ = angle
$O'' C D'$, and therefore
$O' C'$ is parallel to $O C O''$;
and therefore by Arts. 1

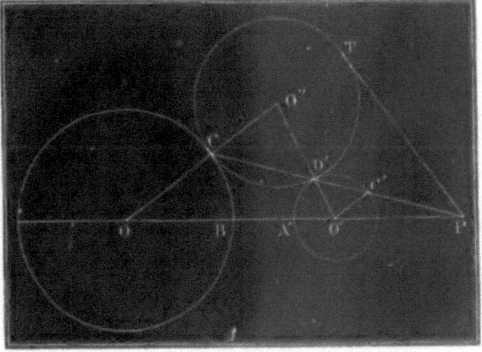

Fig. 3.

and 3, $C D'$ passes through P, and $P T^2 = P C \times P D'$ is constant,
P being here the external centre of similitude of the two fixed circles O and O', and $P T$ being a tangent to the variable circle O''.

Cor. 1. Hence if a variable circle O'' touch two fixed circles O
and O', it will also cut orthogonally another fixed circle whose
centre is P and rad. $= P T$; and therefore conversely, if a variable
circle touch a fixed circle, and cut another fixed circle orthogonally,
it must also touch another fixed circle.

Note. If the variable circle touched one of the two given circles
externally, and the other internally, then the point P' through
which the chord of contact always passes would obviously be the
internal centre of similitude of the two given circles; but in all
other cases P will be the centre of similitude.

Cor. 2. If the two given circles touch each other externally at
B, so that A' coincides with B, then P must be the external centre
of similitude, and the tangent $P T$ to the variable circle will be
equal to $P B$, since by Art. 3, Obs., $P B^2$ is then equal to $P C \times P D'$
$= P T^2$. But if the two given circles touched each other internally
at B, then by the foregoing Note, the line $C D'$ joining the points

of contact will pass through their internal centre of similitude P', and the tangent from P' to the variable circle will then too be equal $P'B$.

Cor. 3. If one of the given circles becomes very large, its circumference becomes nearly straight, as in Art. 4; and hence if a variable circle touch a given straight line and a given circle, the chord of contact will pass through a fixed point on the circumference of the given circle, and the tangent from this point to the variable circle will be constant, which could be easily otherwise demonstrated directly.

Cor. 4. If another circle O''' also touch the two circles O and O' at c and d', then by this Art. 6, $c\,d'$ must also pass through P, the centre of similitude of O and O', and the tangent from P to circle O''' will be equal $P\,T$ the tangent from P to O'', and therefore, by Art. 5, P must be a point on the radical axis of O'' and O'''. Hence this theorem, namely, *If each of two circles touch (in the same way) another pair of circles, the centre of similitude of either pair lies upon the radical axis of the other pair ;* if each of the pair of circles O'', O''' touches one circle of the other pair (O, O') externally, and the other circle internally, then (by Note, Art. 6) P would be the internal centre of similitude of O and O'; but in all other cases P will be their external centre of similitude.

Cor. 5. If we conceive the circle O''' to remain fixed, as well as the two given circles O and O', and O'' alone to vary, then, by the preceding Cor. 4, the centre of similitude Q of O'' and O''' must lie upon the radical axis AB of O and O'; let d and x be the distances of AB from the centres of O''' and O''; then by Art. 1, rad. of O'' : rad. of $O''' = Q\,O'' : Q\,O'''$, therefore by similar angles equal $x : d$; or rad. of $O'' : x =$ rad. of $O''' : d$, and hence we have the following most useful and important theorem ; namely, *If a variable circle touch two fixed circles, its radius varies as the distance of its centre from the radical axis of the given circles ;* and therefore conversely, if a variable circle touch a given circle, and cut a given straight line at a given angle, or, more generally, if its radius vary as the distance of its centre from a given straight line, it shall also touch another given circle.

I shall here give a few remarkable applications of the foregoing useful theorem.

1st. Let OBD be a quadrant, and C the centre of circle LEG inscribed in it, and let n be the centre of the circle PFm touching the two former and the radius OB; then $PO = 7$ times Pn.

For the circle $L'EG'$, inscribed in the adjacent quadrant, OBD' will obviously be equal to circle C, and touch it in E, and OC' will be parallel to the tangent LK, as both are perpendicular to OL. Complete the rectangle $HLKn$, and produce Hn to M and N; then as (by Art. 5, Cor.) LK is the radical axis of

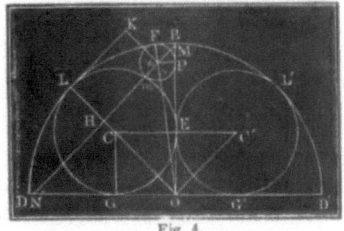

Fig. 4.

circles O and C, which are both touched (in the same sort of way) by circles n and C'; therefore, by the foregoing theorem, Cor. 5, $nK : nP = OL : C'E$; and as $OL = OC + CE$ is the sum of the side and diagonal of a square, GE, whose side $CE = C'E$; therefore nK must equal the side and diagonal of a square described on nP, and therefore equal to $nP + nM$, since MPn, OHN, OCC' are obviously isosceles right-angled triangles. Now, as $OF = OL$, therefore $On — OH = HL — nF = nK — nP$, and therefore $= nM = HM — Hn$; that is, equals $OH — Hn$. Thus the three sides of the right-angled triangle nHO are in arithmetical progression, and therefore they are to each other as 3, 4, and 5. But $nN = nH + HO$ and $nM = HO — Hn$; hence, then, $nN : nM = 4 + 3 : 4 — 3$, that is, equal $7 : 1$; but $PO : Pn = PO : PM$; and therefore by similar triangles $= nN : nM = 7 : 1$.

Cor. The point of contact m is four times as far from OD as from OB. For if Cmn produced, meet OB in R, then by similar triangles RCE, RnP, we get $RC:Rn = CE:nP$; that is, equals $Cm:mn$; therefore RC is cut harmonically at m and n, and so RC, Rm, Rn are in harmonic progression, and therefore CE, mm', and nP, which are proportional to them, are also in harmonic progression, mm' being perpendicular to OB; and therefore their reciprocals, namely, $\dfrac{OR}{CE}$, $\dfrac{OR}{mm'}$ and $\dfrac{OR}{nP}$ are in arithmetical progression; and of course they will remain so still when diminished by the equals $\dfrac{RE}{CE} = \dfrac{Rm'}{mm'} = \dfrac{RP}{nP}$; that is, $\dfrac{OE}{CE}$, $\dfrac{Om'}{mm'}$ and $\dfrac{OP}{nP}$ are in arithmetical progression, and as $\dfrac{OE}{CE}$ is obviously equal 1, and $\dfrac{OP}{nP}$ was proved equal 7, therefore $\dfrac{Om'}{mm'}$ must equal 4.

The foregoing demonstration is easier than and preferable to that inserted by me in "*The Educational Times*" for June, 1857. The celebrated Thomas Simpson first discovered this theorem ($OP = 7 \times Pn$), and gave, in page 284 of his Algebra, an algebraical demonstration of it which is excessively complicated with surd reductions.

2d. Let circles O and O' touch the ordinate CD, and the semi-

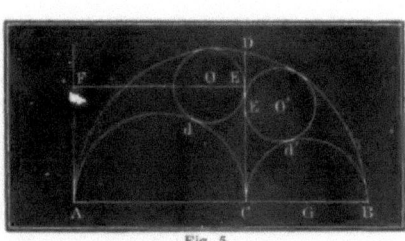

Fig. 5.

circles ADB, AdC, and $Bd'C$. I say circle O = circle O'. For the tangent AF is the radical axis of circles ADB and AdC, both of which are touched by the circles O and $Bd'C$, whose centre is G; draw EOF parallel to AB, through the centre O and the point of contact E, then by foregoing Cor. 5, $OF:OE = GA:GB \therefore EF:2OE = AB:BC$; and as $EF = AC \therefore \dfrac{AC \times BC}{AB} = 2OE$; that is, the diameter of circle O is one half a harmonic mean between $A C$ and $B C$; and the same value would obviously be found for the diameter of circle O'.

NOTE. It is easy to prove that $C D^2 = C E^2 + C E'^2$, and $C E \times C E' = C D \times$ the diameter of O or O'.

3d. Again, let $O B L D$ be a quadrant, $O O'$ its circumscribed square, $D F G O$ and $B H G E$ semicircles whose centres are C and P touching each other in G, and A the centre of a circle touching the three former; then rad. $P B$ $= \frac{1}{3} O B$, and rad. $A L = \frac{1}{6} O B$, and G will be twice as far from $O D$ as from $O B$, and $A C O P$ will be a rectangle. For as $D O'$ is the radical axis of the circles whose centres

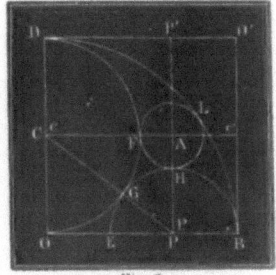

Fig. 6.

are O and C, which are both touched by the circles P and C' ($O C'$ being taken equal and opposite to $O C$), and as $C' O = \frac{1}{3} C' D \therefore$ by Cor. 5, the rad. of $P = \frac{1}{3}$ of P's distance from $D O'$; that is, $P B = \frac{1}{3} O D = \frac{1}{3} O B$; and rad. of $A = \frac{1}{3}$ of A's distance from $D O'$; hence $O B$ is trisected at P and E. Now, the distances of G from $O D$ and $O B$ are obviously equal the distances of $C G P$ from O and E; and therefore the former is double the latter, since $P O = 2 P E$. Again: as $B O'$ is the radical axis of circles O and P, which are both touched by the circles C and A, and as the radius of C is obviously $= \frac{1}{2}$ of C's distance from $B O'$; therefore, by Cor. 5, the radius of $A = \frac{1}{2}$ of A's distance from $B O'$. Now draw $c c'$ and $p p'$ through A parallel to the sides of the square, and therefore equal to them. Therefore $A c' = 2 A L$, and $A p' = 3 A L$, and therefore $O L — A L$, $O B — A c'$, and $O D — A p'$; that is, $O A$, $A c$, $c O$ are in arithmetical progression, and, as they form a right-angled triangle, therefore they are to each other as 3, 4, 5. Hence if $R =$ radius of O, and $r =$ rad. of A, $R — 2 r : R — 3 r = 4 : 3$, which gives $R = 6 r$;

and so Ac (or Op) $= R - 2r \therefore = \frac{2}{3} R = OP$, and Ap (or Oc) $=$ $R - 3r \therefore = \frac{1}{2} R = OC$; so the points c and p coincide with C and P, and therefore $ACOP$ is a rectangle.

4th. Again: if the circle whose centre is A touch the quadrant BLD, and the semicircles described upon its limiting radii OB, OD, then .

   rad. of A : rad. of $BLD = \sqrt{2} - 1 : 3\sqrt{2} - 1 = 1 : 5 + 2\sqrt{2}$.

Since the radical axis of each pair of three circles meets in one

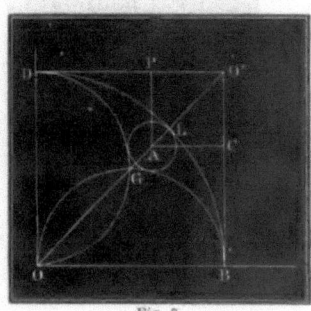

point, therefore the chord OG must pass through the opposite corner of the circumscribed square OO'; and it is evident that the centre A and the point of contact L will lie on OGO'. Complete the square $ACO'P$, and for the reasons assigned in the foregoing (3d), AC or $AP = 3$ times rad. AL.

Fig. 7.

$\therefore AO' = AP\sqrt{2} \therefore = 3AL\sqrt{2}$,

and $\therefore AL(3\sqrt{2} - 1) = LO' = OO' - OL = OB(\sqrt{2} - 1)$; hence $AL : OB = \sqrt{2} - 1 : 3\sqrt{2} - 1$; or $\therefore OB = AL(5 + 2\sqrt{2})$. See Ques. 351 of Colenso's Trigonometry.

5th. If the semicircles on the diameters AB, AC, touching each other at A, be both touched by the circles whose centres are O and O', which touch each other at T; demit OF and $O'G$ perpendiculars on ACB; then if $OF = n$ times diameter of O, $O'G$ will be equal $(n+1)$ times diameter of O', O' being nearer to A than O is. For, by

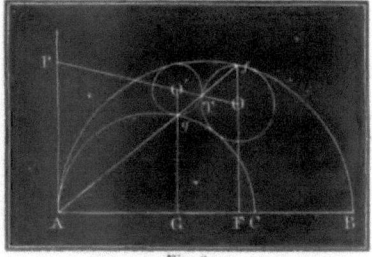

Fig. 8.

Art. 6, Cor. 4, the centre of similitude P of O and O' will lie upon the radical axis of the semicircles on AB, AC, which is their common tangent AP at their point of contact A (Art. 5, Cor.); and as (by Art. 6, Cor. 2), $PA = PT$, $\therefore$ by similar triangles $O'T = O'g$ and $Of = OT$, f and g being the points where AF cuts OF and $O'G$; f and g must therefore be upon the peripheries of circles O and O'. Now, by similar triangles, $Ff : Gg = AF : AG = PO : PO'$, $\therefore$ by Art. $1 = Of : O'g$, and $\therefore Ff + Of : 2\,Of = Gg + O'g : 2\,O'g$; that is, $Of + 2\,Of : 2\,Of = O'G : 2\,O'g$; and as by the hypothesis $OF = n$ times $2\,Of$ $\therefore$ $OF + 2\,Of = (n+1)$ times $2\,Of$; and hence also $O'G = (n+1)$ times $2\,O'g$. The same proof holds true if the two original semicircles touched each other externally at A.

Cor. As the semicircle on diameter BC touches the two given semicircles, and as the distance of its centre from AB is zero, or $= 0$ times its diameter, therefore, if circle whose centre is O, touches these three semicircles, the distance of its centre from AB will be equal its diameter; and thence, if the circle whose centre is O' touch the circle O and any two of the three semicircles, the distance of its centre from AB will be twice its diameter, and if the circle whose centre is O'' touch the circle O' and touch the same two of the three semicircles that O' touches, then the distance of O'' from AB will be three times diameter of circle O'', and so on.

The preceding beautiful theorem, so remarkable for elegance and generality, was known to the ancient geometers under the name of Ἄρβηλος, or, *The Shoemaker's Knife.*

Scholium. When one of the two original semicircles becomes infinite, the truth of the theorem follows at once from the principle, that the common tangent to two circles that touch each other is a mean proportional between their diameters. For, let the circle whose diameter is A and its tangent at A be touched by the circles whose diameters are d_1, d_2, d_3, which touch each other consecutively, B, C, and D being their points of contact with their common tangent, then $AB^2 = \Delta d_1$, $AC^2 = \Delta d_2$; and $BC^2 = d_1 d_2$; there-

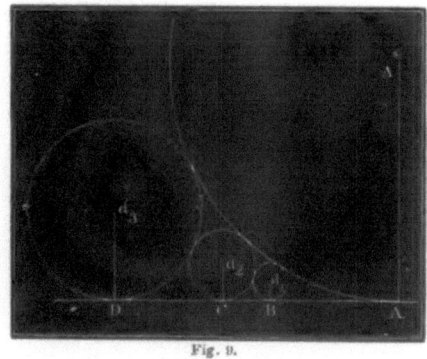

fore $\dfrac{AB^2 \times BC^2}{AC^2} = d_1^2$ and

$\dfrac{AC^2 \times BC^2}{AB^2} = d_2^2$, $\therefore \dfrac{AB}{d_1} = \dfrac{AC}{BC}$

and $\dfrac{AC}{d_2} = \dfrac{AB}{BC}$ and as $\dfrac{AC}{BC} =$

$\dfrac{AB+BC}{BC} = \dfrac{AB}{BC} + 1$, hence

if $\dfrac{AC}{d_2} = n$, $\dfrac{AB}{d_1}$ will be $=$

$n + 1$, which proves the the-

orem in this particular case.

Fig. 9.

REMARK. Since also $AD^2 = \Delta d_3$, and $CD^2 = d_2 d_3$, $\therefore AB^2 \times CD^2 = \Delta d_1 d_2 d_3$, $\therefore = AD^2 \times BC^2$, and therefore $AB \times CD = AD \times BC$, so that AD is cut harmonically at B and C, and therefore $AC \times BD = 2 AB \times CD$, and therefore $BD^2 = \dfrac{4 AB^2 \times CD^2}{AC^2}$, that is $= \dfrac{4 \Delta d_1 d_2 d_3}{\Delta d_2} = 4 d_1 d_3$, which remarkable relation between the diameters of the two circles and their common tangent holds true, in general, for the two circles that can be described touching any three circles that touch each other. I proposed this remarkable theorem in an old number of " *The Educational Times*;" but no geometrical demonstration of the general case has yet appeared. The foregoing particular case is that in which one of the three circles that touch each other becomes infinite.

21 EDEN QUAY, DUBLIN, IRELAND, February 26, 1859.

NOTE. — We commend this very interesting article to the attention of our readers. Its fundamental propositions depend so directly upon the Elements of Geometry as given in all our text-books, that it will be read with ease by all. Those who wish to pursue this subject, including the more general problem of contact, will find it treated by the following authors: PAPPUS, VIETA, DESCARTES, NEWTON, EULER and FUSS (*Memoirs de l'Acad. de Pétersbourg*, 1788); MONGE, (*Correspondance sur l'École*

Polyt., tomes I. et II.) ; GAULTIER DE TOURS (*Journal de l'Ecole Polyt.* 1813) ; GER-
GONNE (*Memoires de l'Acad. de Turin*, 1814, *Annales de Math.*, tomes IV., VII., XI.) ;
DURRANDE and PONCELET (*Annales de Math.*, tome XI.), LESLIE, PUISSANT, STEINER
(CRELLE's *Journal*, tome I., *Annales de Math.*, tome XVII) ; *Library of Useful Knowledge*, Vol. on Geometry, ALVORD (Smithsonian Contributions). This list, which is by
no means complete, shows the amount of research which has been devoted to this subject by many of the ablest geometers.

The term, *Centre of Similitude*, was introduced by MONGE, and that of *Radical
Axis* by GAULTIER DE TOURS.

In regard to the theorem 5th, page 276, it may be stated that a paper on this
subject was read March 9th, 1858, before the American Academy of Arts and Sciences,
by Mr. J. B. HENCK. In this paper, which is mentioned in the Proceedings of the
Academy, and which will probably appear in its Memoirs, the above theorem, with
other properties of tangent circles, is demonstrated and extended to the case in which
one of the fixed circles is tangent to the other externally, as well as to the case in
which it becomes a straight line.

It may be remarked also, that PAPPUS, in Book IV., Theorem XV., of his *Mathe-
maticæ Collectiones*, demonstrates that (COLLINS' Fig. 8, page 276), $OF + 2\,Of$:
$2\,Of :: O'\,G : 2\,O'g$, which, if $OF = n \times 2\,Of$, becomes $n \times 2\,Of + 2\,Of : 2\,Of ::
n + 1 : 1 :: O'\,G : 2\,O'g$. Of this interesting theorem PAPPUS gave two special cases
worthy of note. (1) If $n = 0, 1, 2, 3$, &c., we obtain the corollary on page 277, the
case in which the first of the series of inscribed tangent circles is described on BC as a
diameter. This case is PAPPUS' Theorem XVI., and was referred to by him as the
Arbelos. (2) If $n = \frac{1}{2}, \frac{3}{2}, \frac{5}{2}$, &c., we have the case in which the first circle is tangent
to BC, which is PAPPUS' Theorem XVIII.

It is a little singular, that LESLIE, devoted as he was to the ancient geometry, while
demonstrating the first of these cases, should have entirely omitted the second, which is
equally remarkable.

In GILL's *Mathematical Miscellany*, a problem is given which requires the sum of
the areas of all the inscribed tangent circles. Solutions are given by the Editor, and Dr.
THEODORE STRONG, both of which incidentally develop many interesting properties.

NOTE ON THE COURSING JOINT CURVE OF AN OBLIQUE ARCH IN THE FRENCH SYSTEM.

BY DEVOLSON WOOD, C. E.,
Assistant Professor of Engineering in the University of Michigan.

THE equation of the curve, as given by me in the March number
of the MONTHLY, should contain $\dfrac{1}{\sin \theta}$ as a factor, instead of cot θ.

The differential triangle $a\,b\,c$ is right-angled at c, instead of b, and hence we should have

$$\frac{b\,c}{a\,c} = \frac{r\,d\,\varphi}{d\,s} = \tan i.$$

But to find the equation in terms of x instead of s, let a right

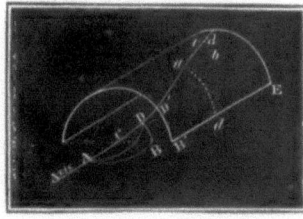 section be made through b, and the angle which this section makes with the section parallel to the face is θ. Hence $b\,d$, which is the perpendicular of the right-angled triangle $a\,b\,d$, equals $\dfrac{b\,c}{\cos\theta} = \dfrac{r\,d\,\varphi}{\cos\theta}$.

$$\therefore \qquad \frac{b\,d}{a\,b} = \frac{r\,d\,\varphi}{\cos\theta\,d\,x} = \tan i = \sin\varphi\,\tan\theta,$$

which gives

$$d\,x = \frac{r\,d\,\varphi}{\sin\theta\,\sin\varphi};$$

or by integration

$$x = \frac{r}{\sin\theta}(\log\tan\tfrac{1}{2}\,\varphi - \log\tan\tfrac{1}{2}\,\varphi_1).$$

Now, for $\varphi_1 =$ any finite value, x will have some finite value for $\varphi = \frac{\pi}{2}$; hence every coursing joint will pass through the crown, if sufficiently prolonged. Take the origin of coördinates such that the initial value of $\varphi_1 = \frac{\pi}{2}$, and the equation becomes

$$x = \frac{r}{\sin\theta}\log\tan\tfrac{1}{2}\,\varphi.$$

If φ_1 be the superior limit, the equation will become

$$x = \frac{r}{\sin\theta}(\log\tan\tfrac{1}{2}\,\varphi_1 - \log\tan\tfrac{1}{2}\,\varphi).$$

Now if $\varphi_1 = \frac{\pi}{2}$, we have

$$x = -\frac{r}{\sin\theta}\log\tan\tfrac{1}{2}\,\varphi = \frac{r}{\sin\theta}\log\cot\tfrac{1}{2}\,\varphi,$$

which is the same as that given on page 210; and only lacks the constant of integration.

EQUATION OF THE COURSING JOINT CURVE.

BY WILLIAM G. PECK,

Adjunct Professor of Mathematics in Columbia College, New York.

THE equation of the developed "coursing joint curve" may be found as follows: Assuming the figure and general notation of page 209, we have for the equation of a developed ring joint,

$$(1) \qquad y = a \mp r \operatorname{versin} \varphi \sin \theta,$$

in which a is arbitrary, corresponding to any ring joint. The upper sign corresponds to the case represented in the figure in which the arch skews to the right, and the lower one to the case in which it skews to the left. There will consequently be two equations. The equation of the developed coursing joint will be of the form

$$(2) \qquad f(x, \varphi) = 0.$$

Differentiating (1) we find

$$(3) \qquad \frac{dy}{d\varphi} = \mp r \sin \theta \sin \varphi.$$

The condition that the curves (1) and (2) are to be normal to each other requires that

$$r^2 + \frac{dy}{d\varphi} \times \frac{dx}{d\varphi} = 0,$$

or substituting for $\dfrac{dy}{d\varphi}$ its value taken from (3), we have

$$r^2 \mp r \sin \theta \sin \varphi \frac{dx}{d\varphi} = 0,$$

whence

$$dx = \pm \frac{r}{\sin \theta} \cdot \frac{d\varphi}{\sin \varphi}.$$

Taking the upper sign and integrating, we have

$$x = \frac{r}{\sin \theta} \log \tan \tfrac{1}{2}\varphi + c.$$

Taking the lower sign and integrating, we have

$$x = \frac{r}{\sin \theta} \log \cot \tfrac{1}{2}\varphi + c.$$

The latter equation is the same as that on page 210.

REMARKS UPON CAYLEY'S (SUPPOSED) NEW THEOREM OF SPHERICAL TRIGONOMETRY.

BY W. CHAUVENET,

Professor of Mathematics in the United States Naval Academy, Annapolis, Md.

THE February number of the *Philosophical Magazine* contains a note by Mr CAYLEY, in which he gives as *new*, the following equation or theorem of Spherical Trigonometry :

$$\sin b \sin c + \cos b \cos c \cos A = \sin B \sin C - \cos B \cos C \cos a,$$

and the March number of the same magazine contains a demonstration of the theorem by the Astronomer Royal. Mr. CAYLEY gives an analytical demonstration of it; Mr. AIRY, a geometrical or semi-geometrical demonstration.

It is remarkable that a standard work like CAGNOLI's *Trigonometrie*, published in French, in 1808, should be so little known in England that this theorem, which is the especial property of CAGNOLI, should, after half a century, be treated as new by mathematicians like CAYLEY and AIRY. Not only does CAGNOLI give the theorem (in Art. 1139 of his Trigonometrie) together with its demonstration ; but he also makes an application of it (in Art. 1135 of the same work) to the solution of the problem of finding the aberration in declination of the fixed stars.

But the theorem might have been found also in DELAMBRE's *Astronomie* (Vol. I., Chap. X., Art. 77), where it is ascribed to CAGNOLI, but differently proved. It is a singular coincidence, that CAYLEY's analytical demonstration is essentially the same as CAGNOLI's; and AIRY's geometrical demonstration the same as DELAMBRE's.

There is one property of this equation which deserves notice here, although it is sufficiently obvious to have attracted the attention of others. It is, that if one member of it is applied to the polar triangle, it gives the other member ; that is, *either member is a function which has the same value in the given spherical triangle and in its polar triangle.* Thus, if we denote the sides and angles of a spherical triangle by a, b, c, A, B, C, and those of its polar triangle by a', b', c', A', B', C', we have

$$\sin b \sin c + \cos b \cos c \cos A = \sin b' \sin c' + \cos b' \cos c' \cos A'.$$

There are several other such functions in spherics. Thus we have

$$\sin b \sin c \sin^2 A = \sin b' \sin c' \sin^2 A'.$$

If u is a function such that

$$u^2 = \sin s \sin (s - a) \sin (s - b) \sin (s - c),$$

in which $s = \frac{1}{2}(a + b + c)$, and if u' is the same function of the sides of the polar triangle; then

$$u \sin A = u' \sin A'.$$

We have also

$$\cos \frac{a}{2} \sin \frac{B+C}{2} + \sin \frac{a}{2} \cos \frac{B-C}{2} = \cos \frac{a'}{2} \sin \frac{B'+C'}{2} + \sin \frac{a'}{2} \cos \frac{B'-C'}{2},$$

and others of the same kind, which, however, are too complicated to be useful, and are not worth repeating.

A SECOND BOOK IN GEOMETRY.

REASONING UPON FACTS.

BY THOMAS HILL.

[Continued from page 256.]

CHAPTER IV.

ANALYSIS AND SYNTHESIS.

41. WHAT I have called demonstration or deduction, but which is better called synthesis, because it is a putting together, one by one, of the parts of a complex truth, is the only mode of proof that you will usually find in works on geometry. And if such works are carefully read they are always intelligible to a child of good geometrical reasoning powers.

42. But the study of such works does not always teach a child to reason for himself. The pupil says, " Yes, I understand all this, and yet I could not have done it without aid ; I do not see how the writer knew where to begin ; how he knew that by starting from these particular truths, and going on that particular path, he could reach that proposition." A pupil who had never studied geometry could not, for instance, tell why in articles 34–36 we should begin with showing that vertical angles are equal. He would not see any connection between that truth, and the desired proof; and would not know that this synthesis had been preceded, in the mind of the writer, by a rapid analysis, such as that of Arts. 26–31.

43. It is as though a mountain guide, wishing to make for a child a path up to a mountain peak, should lead him along the highway, until the peak was hidden, and then begin boldly to clear a road, through the brush-wood and trees, until he reached the top. The child might say, " How did you dare begin at once to cut down the bushes and clear the path ? How did you know that the road you were making would not lead you to the edge or to the foot of some precipice, or that it would not take you to a different peak from that which you wished to climb ? " And if the child received no answer to his questions, — if he was not told that the guide had already climbed to the summit and again descended, he would have learned little to help him in laying out paths for himself.

44. In like manner, although the descent from difficult propositions to more simple is more tedious than the ascent, it will be more useful to a learner, because it will show him the manner in which, by a mental process, we discover the points from which we are to start in our ascent. This is to say, if we follow a good analysis, we shall learn how to perform synthesis for ourselves ; but if we were simply to follow a writer's synthesis, we should not learn how to analyze, which must nevertheless always go before synthesis.

45. Among the first requisites in reasoning is a clear understanding of the object in view ; that is, of the point to be proved ; and next, a clear perception of each particular part of the demonstration, and of the connection of each part with the adjacent parts.

Thus in laying out a path up a mountain, it is necessary to know exactly from what point you wish to start, and to what point you wish to go. It is also necessary to examine carefully each point of the road, for a single impassable place would destroy the value of the whole road.

46. Each step of the proof must be a simple step, and clearly true ; that is, it must be so simple and self-evident as to be beyond all doubt.

47. The analysis must end, or the synthesis begin, with truths that are self-evident, or else that have been already proved. Your mountain path must begin on level or at least on accessible ground.

48. Care must be taken not to introduce any thing as true which has not been proved. This would be like starting your mountain road in two places at once. You might afterwards find impassable barriers between the two parts of your road, and perhaps find that one of them could not be made to the top of the mountain, nor the other to its base. For example, in Art. 36, I drew a straight line through A, parallel to B C: This was very well — for no one can possibly doubt such a line might be drawn. But if, instead of that I had said, let us draw a straight line through A in such a manner as to make the angles on the two sides of A equal to the angles B and C, I should have done what I had no right to do. For that would be taking for granted a thing which I must prove : namely, that a straight line can be thus drawn. It would be starting half way up my mountain, and taking for granted that the lower part of the path could be built afterwards.

49. Whether we reason by synthesis or analysis, we must therefore reason very carefully,

in order to connect the proposition which we wish to prove by a stairway of self-evident steps with a self-evident foundation.

50. By a self-evident truth, I mean a truth which cannot be made any plainer, and which is already perfectly plain to an intelligent person who looks steadily at it. For instance, that two straight lines can cross each other only once; that any curve can be cut by a straight line in at least two places; that either side of a triangle is shorter than the sum of the other two; that if three strings, and no more than three, come from one point, one of them must have an end at that point; these are self-evident truths.

51. By a self-evident step in reasoning, I mean the statement of the relation of one truth to another, or of the dependence of one truth upon another, when that dependence or that relation is itself a self-evident truth. Self-evident steps in reasoning are simply the statement of self-evident truths of connection. For instance, when we have explained the meaning of "a straight line" by calling it a line that has in every part the same direction, and have explained the meaning of an angle by the difference of two directions in one plane, then it follows that the angle which two straight lines make with each other is the c same in one part of the lines as in any other; and that the two different angles apparently made by two straight lines cannot really be made, unless one of the lines goes in two opposite directions at the same time. No reasoning can make the connection between these definitions and the equality of vertical angles any more plain. It is a self-evident connection.

52. Or, suppose that we say that you cannot make one rope go from a centre post to the four corners of a square, and also around the square, and have but a single rope from post to post. We should prove it in this way. Let there be a rope around the square, and going also from each post to the centre. This of course can be imagined. It is a definite and allowable conception. But we will also prove that this rope must be in two pieces. For each of the four corners will have three lines coming from it, one towards each adjacent corner, and one towards the centre. Thus it follows by self-evident connection, from the conception of the rope going around the square and to each corner, that there will be four points, from each of which three lines come. But it is a self-evident truth that at each of these points there must be one end of the rope. Hence, by self-evident connection, there will be four ends of rope about the square. Hence, by self-evident connection with the self-evident truth that one piece of rope can have but two, and must have two, ends, it follows that there must be two pieces of rope, and cannot be only one. Now the whole of this proof is simply the statement of self-evident connections between the proposition that one rope cannot go around a square and also from each corner to the centre without doubling, and the self-evident truths that a piece of rope must have two, and cannot have more than two, ends; and that when only three lines of rope come from one point, one of them must end at that point. The proof is simple; and yet intelligent men have spent hours in experimenting with a string and five posts thus arranged; or with a pencil and five dots representing posts.

53. Many self-evident truths are general, and self-evident steps are generally the recognition of general relations; and therefore most writers on reasoning, say that reasoning consists simply in showing that a particular case comes under a general class. But in the mathematics, there are many self-evident truths which it is difficult to state in a general form; and I therefore think that the explanation which I have given of the process of reasoning, will be of more use to you in your geometrical studies.

Mathematical Monthly Notices.

Elements of Mechanics ; for the Use of Colleges, Academies, and High Schools. By WIL-
LIAM G. PECK, M. A., Adjunct Professor of Mathematics, Columbia College. New York :
A. S. Barnes & Burr, 51 and 53 John Street. 1859.

THE standard the author of this work had in mind, though not the method of demonstration employed in its preparation, is sufficiently obvious from the title-page, even if his preface
had not contained the formal statement that it is intended to occupy middle ground between
works on Natural Philosophy of mere description, without any attempt at rigorous demonstration, and those demanding considerable knowledge of the higher mathematics.

The question which at once suggested itself to us was, ought the author to have used the
principles of the calculus ? If it was intended that the work should be studied after the
Elements of the calculus, there could be no question about it. But if, on the other hand,
it is to be put into the hands of those who have not studied the calculus, however thoroughly
they may have mastered the more elementary branches, then it is as certain that the calculus
should not be used. The author has, therefore, in using the calculus in the chapters " On
the Centre of Gravity," " On Motion," &c., limited the use of his work by so doing. We
should regret this the less, if we felt less pleased with it. When the elements of the higher
mathematics are as generally studied as they should be, in our institutions of learning, then Prof.
PECK's work will be well adapted for the use of Colleges, Academies, and High Schools. Now,
as a whole, it is only adapted for use in those institutions in which the study of the calculus is a
part of the required course, and is taught to all ; but this is less a criticism of the book than of
the present mathematical standard in our system of education.

In deciding what subjects to introduce, in what order to arrange them, and how general
a discussion to give them, we think the author has shown good judgment. If, in the few cases
investigated by the calculus, an analysis had been used which the student of elementary geometry or algebra could comprehend, and the demonstrations, at present in the text, were in the
margin, thus adapting the work to both classes of pupils, we hardly know in what other respect
it could be materially improved ; unless it be, as it seems to us, to add under each head a few
more difficult examples to the judicious selection already given. The calculus is an elective
study in some of our best colleges, and when such is the case but few indeed elect it. In academies and high schools, the study is always elective, so far as we know, and never studied at
all in such institutions, unless the teacher happens to be a good mathematician himself, and is
ambitious to teach a whole course of pure mathematics ; and even in such a very favorable
case, only a very small class at best can usually be found prepared to take it. To be sure,
only its very first and simplest principles are used in the book before us ; but this does not
in the least remove the difficulty, since the notation even of the calculus is peculiar, and its
fundamental conceptions equally new to one whose mathematical knowledge is confined to
the simpler elements of mathematics. We know it has been, and is still, a question with good
teachers of mathematics, whether it is better for the student, when the subject demands
the calculus, to take a work which avoids it by resort to methods, which, however general
they may be in their character and uniform in their application, no one conversant with the

calculus would ever think of using as a means of investigation; or whether he will not in the end be by far the gainer in all respects by first mastering the elements of the calculus, and afterwards using it in all investigations demanding the infinitesimal analysis. WEISBACH'S *Treatise on Mechanics and Engineering*, in which the calculus is not used, but in which ability of a high order, with large experience, is taxed to furnish the best possible substitute, is a good case in point. We are free to admit, that we should much prefer, and we think it would be altogether best for the student, to teach him the calculus first, and then a WEISBACH written in its language and symbols; and we hope yet to see this branch much more generally studied in our schools, and introduced much earlier in the course. But this is hardly to be expected so long as the standard for admission to college is so low, and especially as compared with the ancient languages. This inequality in the preparatory course is even more unfortunate for the mathematics after than before admission to college.

A Tract on the Possible and Impossible Cases of Quadratic Duplicate Equalities in the Diophantine Analysis: To which is added a short but comprehensive Appendix, in which most of the useful and important Propositions in the Theory of Numbers are very concisely demonstrated. By MATTHEW COLLINS, B. A., Senior Moderator in Mathematics and Physics, and Bishop Law's Mathematical Prizeman, Trinity College, Dublin.

The following synopsis of the Contents of this Tract will give the best idea of its character; and to those of our readers interested in this department of analysis we most heartily commend it.

The possible and impossible cases of the following sets of two simultaneous equations are treated, namely:

CHAP. I. $x^2 + a y^2$ and $x^2 - a y^2 =$ squares.

CHAP. II. $x^2 + y^2$ and $x^2 + a y^2 =$ squares.

CHAP. III. $x^2 + y^2$ and $x^2 - a y^2 =$ squares.

By one uniform method it is proved that the first set is impossible for all integer values of a less than 20, except 5, 6, 7, 13, 14, or 15; the second set is impossible for any integer values of a between 1 and 20, except 7, 10, 11, or 17; and the third set for any integer values of a between 1 and 18, except 7 or 11. General formulas are given, much shorter than FERMAT's method, for finding any number of solutions in integers prime to each other.

Chapter II. also contains a scholium, giving very extensive and important additions to the few cases in which the equation

$$a x^4 + b x^2 y^2 + c y^4 = \text{a square},$$

was heretofore known and proved to be impossible by FERMAT and EULER.

The Tract closes with a list of over three hundred and fifty subscribers, including the names of HAMILTON, GRAVES, JELLETT, LARDNER, WOOLHOUSE, and others, well known in this country; and those wishing to procure it will consult the third page of cover.

Editorial Items.

THE following gentlemen have sent us solutions of the Prize Problems in the February number of the MONTHLY: —

GEORGE B. HICKS, Student, Cleveland, Ohio, answered all the questions.

ARTHUR H. WRIGHT, Senior Class, Yale College, answered all the questions. (H. A. NEWTON, Prof.)

JOHN Y. BEDINGFIELD, Student, Bowdon Collegiate Institution, Bowdon, Carroll Co., Ga., answered all the questions. (JOHN M. RICHARDSON, Prof. Math.)

A Student in Union Square Academy, Baltimore, Md., answered all the questions but III. (JOHN MCNEVIN, Prof.)

ASHER B. EVANS, Junior Class, Madison University, Hamilton, New York, answered all the questions. (L. M. OSBORN, Prof.)

WILLIAM E. MERRILL, Cadet, First Class, U. S. Military Academy, West Point, N. Y., answered all the questions. (A. E. CHURCH, Prof.)

WALLER HOLLADAY, Student of Mathematics in the University of Virginia, answered all the questions. (A. T. BLEDSOE, Prof.)

F. RICHARDSON, Junior Class, Haverford College, Delaware Co., Pa., answered all but questions III and V. (M. C. STEVENS, Prof.)

JOHN R. MEIGS, Junior Class, Columbian College, Washington, D. C., answered all but questions III and V. (EDWARD T. FRISTOE, Prof.)

GEORGE A. OSBORNE, Jr., Student in the Lawrence Scientific School, answered all the questions. (H. L. EUSTIS, Prof.)

DAVID TROWBRIDGE, Student, Perry City, Schuyler Co., N. Y., answered all the questions but I.

ISAAC H. HALL, Senior Class, Hamilton College, Clinton, N. Y., answered all the questions. (OREN ROOT, Prof.)

GEORGE W. JONES, Jr., Senior Class, Yale College, answered all the questions. (H. A. NEWTON, Prof.)

It gives us pleasure to add the following names to our list of co-perators and contributors: S. E. BENJAMIN, Esq., Patten, Me.; JAMES CLARK, Esq., Wayne, Me.; THOMAS P. STOWELL, Esq., Hornellsville, Steuben Co., N. Y.; CHARLES D. LAWRENCE, Professor of Mathematics, Bethel College, Russellville, Ky.; BENJAMIN ALVORD, Major U. S. Army, Fort Vancouver, Washington Territory; Dr. WILLIAM J. WALLER, President of Shelby College, Shelbyville, Ky.; JOHN BORDEN, Esq., Chicago, Ill.; Rev. ANTHONY VALLAZ, Phil. Dr., Late Ordinary Professor of Mathematics in the Royal University of Pesth, New Orleans, La.; JOHN A. NICHOLS, Professor of Mixed Mathematics in the Free Academy, New York City; ADOLPH WERNER, Esq., N. Y. Free Academy. . . . . . We have more material on hand accepted for publication, than is contained in the eight numbers of the MONTHLY already issued. This will explain why contributions are so often delayed beyond the month for which their authors intended them. This is a matter entirely out of our control, and must remain so, while we are obliged to confine the MONTHLY to its present number of pages per month.